Passover

Story and pictures by **Miriam Nerlove**

ALBERT WHITMAN & COMPANY, MORTON GROVE, ILLINOIS

For Paula and her Seders, with love,
and special thanks to Abby and Karen

Text and illustrations © 1989 by Miriam Nerlove.
Published in 1989 by Albert Whitman & Company,
6340 Oakton Street, Morton Grove, Illinois 60053.
Published simultaneously in Canada by
General Publishing, Limited, Toronto.
Printed in the United States of America.
10   9   8   7   6   5   4   3

Library of Congress Cataloging-in-Publication Data

Nerlove, Miriam.
Passover/written and illustrated by Miriam Nerlove.
        p.   cm.
Summary: Rhyming text and illustrations depict the history of
Passover and one boy's family Seder.
ISBN 0-8075-6360-9 (hardcover)
ISBN 0-8075-6361-7 (paperback)
1. Passover—Juvenile literature. 2. Seder—Juvenile
literature.
[1. Passover. 2. Seder.] I. Title.
BM695.P3N36 1989   89-35393
296.4'37—dc20   CIP
                                                      AC

PASSOVER! It's time for Passover!

The story of Passover began long ago . . .
In Egypt there lived a cruel pharaoh.

Pharaoh gave a royal command—
Jews must be slaves across his land!

He said to Moses, "I'll never free your people from their slavery."

One night the Jewish people fled.
They had no time to make real bread
but took the unbaked dough instead.

Moses brought them to the sea.

The waters parted! Could it be?

Then he led them far away
to freedom—what we have today!

On Passover, each year in spring,
we remember all these things.

First Grandma comes, then Uncle Lou,
Aunt Maxine, and Cousin Sue.

This night we have our family Seder.
We'll read and eat, then read more later.

I ask Four Questions, and we look
for answers in our Seder book.

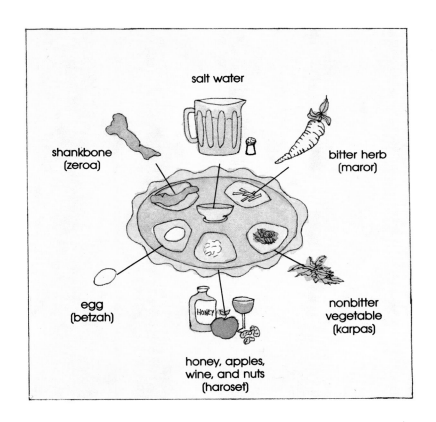

salt water

shankbone
(zeroa)

bitter herb
(maror)

egg
(betzah)

nonbitter
vegetable
(karpas)

honey, apples,
wine, and nuts
(haroset)

The Seder plate is filled with food
to help explain our thankful mood.

Matzah—flat and crunchy bread—
recalls the night our people fled.
We eat it when the blessing's said.

Sue and I get tastes of wine,
but mostly grape juice as we dine.

After dinner, the hunt begins—
who finds the afikoman wins!

I look behind the swinging door . . .

Sue finds it in a kitchen drawer!

I open the front door in case
Elijah comes to take his place.

Then we sing Passover songs.
I know some words and sing along.

It's really late, but that's all right.
Tonight's a very special night!

ABOUT PASSOVER

Passover is a holiday that takes place in spring, beginning on the fifteenth day of the Hebrew month of Nisan (usually April). It celebrates the Jewish people's freedom from four hundred years of slavery in Egypt. When the pharaoh of Egypt refused to let the Jews go, God sent nine plagues, each worse than the last, to force him to change his mind. When Pharaoh still would not free the Jews, God sent a tenth plague: the Angel of Death, who killed the firstborn son in every Egyptian home. The angel "passed over" the Jewish homes. That is why we call this holiday *Passover.*

At last Pharaoh let the Jews go, and led by Moses and his brother Aaron, they fled Egypt. But Pharaoh changed his mind and sent an army that pursued the Jews to the Red Sea. God worked another miracle to save the Jews: He parted the sea, allowing only the Jews to cross safely. The waters then closed in on Pharaoh's army, and they perished. After wandering for forty years in the desert, the Jewish people finally returned to their ancient homeland of Israel.

Some people celebrate Passover for seven days, and others for eight. During this time, it is traditional to remove and not eat bread and other forbidden foods, and to eat unleavened bread called *matzah.* On the first night of the holiday, there is a special *Seder* meal where families and friends gather. (Many homes have another Seder on the second night, too.) Jews read from the *Haggadah,* a book that tells the story of Passover and also explains what to do during the Seder.

As the Seder starts, everyone says a special prayer of hope. They pray that by next year, all people will be able to celebrate freedom. After this prayer, a young child asks the *Four Questions,* which begin, "Why is this night different from all other nights?" The answer is the telling of the Passover story.

During the Seder, certain foods are always eaten. These include *haroset,* a mixture of wine, apples, honey, and nuts that recalls the mortar Jews used in laying bricks for the Egyptians. Bitter herbs (*maror*) bring to mind the bitterness of slavery, and a nonbitter green vegetable, usually parsley (*karpas*), stands for spring and rebirth. The flat, crunchy matzah helps people remember the night the Jewish people fled Egypt without time to bake their bread.

After dinner, the door is opened for the prophet Elijah. According to tradition, he will one day return to announce the coming of the Messiah. The children search for the *afikoman,* a piece of matzah that was hidden at the beginning of the Seder. Special Passover songs are sung, and families and friends draw close together to celebrate not only the freedom of the Jewish people but also the warmth and joy that freedom brings.